TULSA CITY-COUNTY LIBRARY

sbep
n/na
W9-BDP-823

For Max Lerman —S.C.

For Bailey—
whose every sound and movement
is a joyful jazz in our memories
—B.D.

JAZZMATAZZ!

By Stephanie Calmenson

Illustrated by Bruce Degen

HarperCollins*Publishers*

When the weather gets cold
And a mouse slips in,
A jazzmatazz story
Is sure to begin.

You won't hear a bell
Or a knock at the door.
The mouse will come in
Through a crack in the floor.

While you're washing the dishes,
He'll step on your feet,

Then scurry in a hurry
To the piano seat.

You'll scoot him away,
But he's got pizzazz.
He jumps on the keys . . .

And starts to play jazz!

"I plink, *plink*, plink.
How about you?"

Mouse points to Dog,
With his bones and bowl.

"I play my drum with
My heart and soul!"

Doo-dat, diddy-dat,
Diddy-dat, doo!

"I bang-a-bang, bang!
How about you?"

Dog points to Cat,
Who says, "It's no riddle.

You know what *I* play.
I'm the cat with the fiddle."

Doo-dat, diddy-dat,
Diddy-dat, doo!

"I fiddle-dee-dee.
How about you?"

Cat points to Bird,
Who sings, "Tweetily-tweet.
My voice is my music.
Isn't it sweet?"

Doo-dat, diddy-dat,
Diddy-dat, doo!

"I tweetily-tweet.
How about you?"

Bird points to Fish,
Who swims round and round.
"My itty bitty bubbles
Make a blub-blub sound."

"I blub-blub-blub.
How about you?"

When Fish points to me,
Here's what I say,

"I love to sing and
There's plenty that I play!"

"But my feet are tapping
And they just won't stop.
Will you look at me now?

I'll tap *till I drop!*"

Doo-dat, diddy-dat,
Diddy-dat, doo!

"I tap-tap-tapitty.
How about you?"

Come on, everybody.
It's time to join in!
Our jazzmatazz jamming
Will now begin.

Plink, plink.
Bang-a-bang.
Fiddle-dee-dee.
Tweetily-tweet.
Blub-blub.
Tap with me!

Doo-dat, diddy-dat,

Diddy-dat, doo!

DOO-DAT.
DIDDY-

DAT.
DOO!

A Note from the Author and Artist

On a cold winter day, we were on e-mail, chatting about this and that. At some point, we got to talking about the weather.

Bruce: The field mice are coming into our house to get warm.

Stephanie: City mice do the same. I squeak—I mean, speak—from experience.

Bruce: Speaking of squeaking, last night a mouse ran across my foot while I was washing the dishes, then ran under the piano!

Stephanie: Train the mouse to run *on* the piano—and play *jazz*!

Bruce: Therein lies a children's book.

You are now holding that book in your hands.

Diddy-dat, doo!

STEPHANIE CALMENSON BRUCE DEGEN

Jazzmatazz!
Text copyright © 2008 by Stephanie Calmenson
Illustrations copyright © 2008 by Bruce Degen

Manufactured in China.
All rights reserved. No part of this book may be used or reproduced in any manner whatsoever without written permission except in the case of brief quotations embodied in critical articles and reviews. For information address HarperCollins Children's Books, a division of HarperCollins Publishers, 1350 Avenue of the Americas, New York, NY 10019. www.harpercollinschildrens.com

Library of Congress Cataloging-in-Publication Data is available.
ISBN-10: 0-06-077289-1 — ISBN-13: 978-0-06-077289-5
ISBN-10: 0-06-077290-5 (lib. bdg.) — ISBN-13: 978-0-06-077290-1 (lib. bdg.)

Typography by Carla Weise 1 2 3 4 5 6 7 8 9 10 ❖ First Edition